Hilda Crumm's Hats

Linda Hendry

AN ALLIGATOR PRESS BOOK

HarperCollinsPublishersLtd

For Leszek,
who lets me keep most
of the junk I bring home.

An Alligator Press Book
Consulting Editor, Dennis Lee

Published by
HarperCollins Publishers Ltd.
Suite 2900, Hazelton Lanes
55 Avenue Road
Toronto, Canada M5R 3L2

Canadian Cataloguing in Publication Data
Hendry, Linda
    Hilda Crumm's hats

"An Alligator Press book"
ISBN 0-00-648082-9

I. Title.

PS8565.E577H5 1994 jC813'.54 C94-930088-8
PZ7.H45Hi 1994

Hilda Crumm loved junk. Old junk, new junk, broken, chipped or glued junk — Hilda was always bringing home something.

There was junk in her living room,

junk in her bedroom,

and junk in her kitchen.

There was junk everywhere!

Hilda could not have been happier.

But Hilda's neighbors were not very happy, and one day they came knocking at her door. Mrs. Derwin, the superintendent, stepped out from the crowd.

"Hilda," she said, "you know that all of us here at the Windy Arms are very fond of you, but we do not like your junk. That pile on your balcony is getting especially large and we think you should clean it up."

Hilda had to agree. There *were* a lot of things on her balcony. "I guess I should clean up a bit," she said to herself. So she found a broom and some empty boxes and set to work.

Hilda started in the corner with the biggest pile. She was busily pulling out plant pots and carpet samples when a load of junk toppled down and landed right on her head.

Hilda heard a screeching sound. A huge pink car had slammed on its brakes and was backing up the street. The rear window sunk away with an electric whir and a rather pinkish lady poked her head out. A puffy pink poodle popped up beside her.

"Excuse me, my dear," the lady said, "but wherever did you get that darling little hat you're wearing?"

Hilda looked surprised. "Why…ah…I made it myself," Hilda told her.

"Fabulous. Do you suppose you could make one for me?" the lady asked. "I would need it by Friday. I'm going to a very special party."

"I don't see why not," Hilda answered.

"Wonderful. See you Friday." And with that the window rolled up and the car drove away.

So Hilda made a hat. It was very pink,
and it was very popular.

The day after the party, Hilda's phone started ringing. Her hat was a hit.

Percy Fairweather ordered a green hat. Beatrice L'amour wanted a purple hat, and Darnell Rigby, the roving reporter from Channel 10 News ordered a rainhat in red.

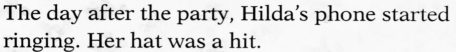

Dougal Macleod, the lead singer for The Electric Bananas, ordered five yellow hats — four hats for the band members...

...and one for his mom.

Before long, everyone who was anyone was wearing a hat by Hilda.

Hilda's apartment was very, very clean. And Hilda's neighbors were very, very happy. But Hilda missed her junk.

Then Hilda had an idea. She grabbed a rusty old baby buggy and a rickety old wagon and off she went.

Hilda's neighbors were very worried.

They were also *very* curious…

...but not for long!